Snow White
& The Seven Dwarfs

Published by

Berryland
Books
www.berrylandbooks.com

Edited by Claire Black
Music composed and performed by Nick Cartledge • Narrated by Katharine Wood

Once upon a time there was a Queen who was very happy because she was about to have her first baby.

One day, as she sat sewing, she pricked her finger.

A drop of blood fell onto the snow and she noticed how pretty it looked.

Soon the Queen gave birth to a beautiful baby girl.

She had skin as white as snow, so the Queen decided to call her Snow White.

Sadly, the Queen died shortly after giving birth.

Snow White was a very happy little girl and grew up to be kind and helpful.

After some time, the King married again and the new Queen was wicked.

She treated Snow White very badly.

The wicked Queen had a magic mirror and every morning she would stand in front of it and ask, "Mirror, mirror, on the wall, who is the fairest of them all?"

The mirror would reply, "You, oh Queen, are the fairest of them all."

Then, one day the mirror replied, "Snow White is the fairest of them all!"

The Queen was furious.

She sent for a huntsman and ordered him to take Snow White deep into the forest and kill her.

To make sure that he did this, the Queen gave him a box in which to bring back her heart.

The huntsman was a kind man who loved Snow White but he was frightened of the wicked Queen.

Then he thought of a plan.

He led Snow White into the forest and told her the Queen's wishes.

He asked Snow White to run away and never return to the palace.

The huntsman then killed a deer and took out its heart to give to the Queen.

The Queen was delighted.

Meanwhile, Snow White ran deeper into the forest.

It was beginning to get very dark and she was lost and scared.

Luckily, some animals who had been watching, came over to help her.

They led Snow White to a little house.

She knocked on the door, but nobody answered.

She pushed the door open and peeped inside.

"What a nice little house this is, but everything is such a mess!" she said.

Snow White thought that if she cleaned up the little house, perhaps she would be allowed to stay.

She washed the floors, dusted the furniture, made the beds and cooked a lovely meal.

All the animals helped her and soon the place was sparkling clean.

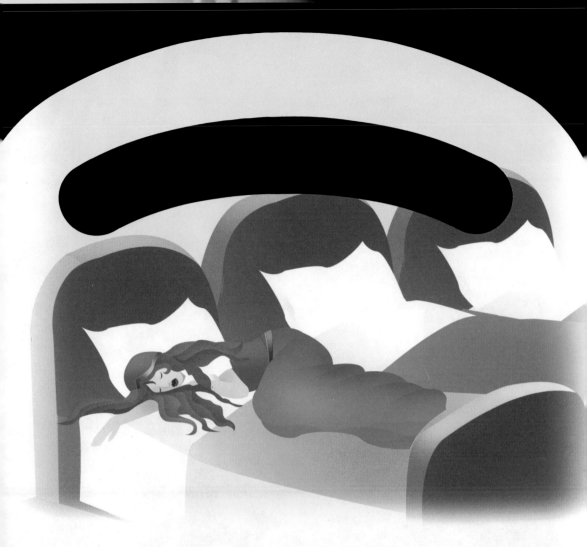

Snow White felt very tired and quickly fell asleep.

Evening came and out of the forest seven little dwarfs appeared.

They were returning to their little home after a busy day working in the mines.

"There's a light coming from our home!" one of the dwarfs shouted.

The dwarfs crept up to the little house and looked inside.

What a surprise they had!

The house was so clean and tidy.

Upstairs they found a beautiful princess sleeping on their beds!

At first they were frightened, but when Snow White woke up they realized how sweet and kind she was.

From that day onwards, Snow White lived happily with the seven dwarfs.

Back in the palace, the Queen stood in front of her magic mirror and asked, "Mirror, mirror on the wall, who is the fairest of them all?"

To her surprise the mirror replied, "Snow White is still the fairest of them all.

She lives in the forest with the seven dwarfs!"

The Queen was very cross and she decided to use her evil powers on Snow White.

She turned herself into an old woman and mixed together a poisonous potion.

Next, the Queen dropped an apple into the poison and it came out a rosy red.

Then she placed the apple in a basket and went into the forest to find Snow White.

Very soon the Queen arrived at the little house and knocked on the door.

Snow White answered and invited the old lady to come in and sit down.

"Please, let me give you something for being so kind," said the Queen and she offered Snow White the poisoned apple.

"Thank you," said Snow White.

She bit into the apple and instantly fell to the floor.

"Now at last, I am the fairest of them all!" screeched the wicked Queen.

That evening, the dwarfs returned to find Snow White lying on the floor.

They placed her body in a glass coffin and took turns to watch over her.

A young prince heard about the beautiful princess in the glass coffin and rode into the forest to find her.

The minute the Prince set eyes upon Snow White, he fell in love with her.

He opened the lid of the glass coffin.

As he lifted her body, the piece of poisoned apple, which had been stuck in her throat, fell away.